The Be

by Jane Rogers • illustrated by Christine Battuz

"I must make a nest.

Who will help?" asked Hen.

"I will help," said Skunk.

Skunk had a box.

"A box is good for a nest."

Fox had a bag of sand.

But sand is not good for a nest.

Ant gave Hen grass.

Bug gave Hen sticks.

"I can use them," said Hen.

Hen went to work.

"I will not rest," said Hen.

"I must be fast."

Skunk and Fox helped.

Ant and Bug helped.

At last Hen had a nest.

Is it a good nest?

"It is the best nest!" said Hen.